W9-AFO-837

Martha Alexander

My Outrageous Friend Charlie

Dial Books for Young Readers · New York

Published by Dial Books for Young Readers
A Division of Penguin Books USA Inc.
2 Park Avenue
New York, New York 10016

Published simultaneously in Canada
by Fitzhenry & Whiteside Limited, Toronto
Printed in Hong Kong by South China Printing Co.
Design by Amelia Lau Carling
First Edition
E
1 3 5 7 9 10 8 6 4 2

Library of Congress Cataloging in Publication Data
Alexander, Martha G.
My outrageous friend Charlie/Martha Alexander.
p. cm.
Summary: Jessie Mae admires her outrageous friend
Charlie because he can do anything, but when
he gives her a Super Delux Triple Magic kit for
her birthday, she finds that she can be outrageous too.
ISBN 0-8037-0587-5. ISBN 0-8037-0588-3 (lib. bdg.)
[1. Friendship—Fiction. 2. Behavior—Fiction.] I. Title.
PZ7.A3777My 1989 [E]—dc19 88-10936 CIP AC

The full-color artwork was prepared using pencil
and watercolor washes. It was then color-separated
and reproduced as red, blue, yellow, and black halftones.

For Malia K.M. with love
and special thanks to J.Z. and her outrageous friend

My friend Charlie is outrageous!
He always gets the tail on the donkey without peeking.

He says it's easy. It's not easy for *me*.

Charlie is good at everything.

He can ride his bike with no hands.
I wouldn't even try.

He says I can do anything I want to do.
I wish I could.

Charlie is the bravest person in the world.
He can dive from the high board.
And he can pick up pennies from the bottom of
the pool. He's my hero.

"Jessie Mae, I don't want to be your hero.
I'm your friend."

For my birthday Charlie gave me a Super Delux
Triple Magic Kit (guaranteed to work).
"You need some magic in your life, Jessie Mae.
Maybe this will help."

First I rubbed the magic cream on my hands.
Then I drank the magic green bubbly juice.
I clapped my hands three times and blinked my
eyes three times. I turned around three times
and there in front of me was a rabbit.

"Make me disappear," said the rabbit. So I did.

Then I clapped my hands three times and the rabbit reappeared.

"What a great magic set this is!
  I wonder what else I can do?" I asked out loud.
  The rabbit said, "Anything you want to do, Jessie Mae."

So I walked up the wall and across the ceiling.

This is really fun. I can do anything I want to do—
just like Charlie said.

I think I'll take a trip around the world. I'd better go tell Charlie.

Charlie looked at me and shook his head.
"Jessie Mae, that's impossible. You can't do that."

I looked Charlie right in the eye and said,
"I can too, Charlie. You wait and see."

I did six cartwheels and jumped right over Charlie's fence. Then I ran home and Charlie ran after me.

"I don't believe what I just saw, Jessie Mae!"

"Believe it, Charlie. Believe it!
I can do anything I want to do.

"Look, I can juggle six apples. It's a breeze!

"I can walk on my hands for as long as I please!

"I can pull a rabbit out of my sleeve!"

"Jessie Mae, how in the world did you do that?"
"It's simple, Charlie. I used my Super Delux
Magic Kit you gave me for my birthday."

"Jessie Mae, there's no such thing as magic. It's just
a bunch of tricks."
"Well, Charlie, just believe what you want to believe.
I'm going on my trip."

"Jessie Mae, wait! Can I go with you?"
"Sure, Charlie, I thought you'd want to go.
  I brought these goggles and this sweater for
  you. It might be cold up there.

"And don't forget to buckle your seat belt, Charlie."
"Jessie Mae, you're outrageous."

"I know."